If you make a mistake, it's never too late to say ~~sory~~.
sorry

Ivy, The Prodigal Daughter
part of the series "Fables, Parables
& Silly Tales with Morals"

Ivy smiled at Mom, "I love you mommy. Also, I need money. GIMME, GIMME, GIMME."

Mom told Ivy. "Oh honey, I love you too but please. You know money's hard to come by and doesn't grow on trees.

"Oh Mom. Stop trying to be so funny.
Now, to the bank machine! It's time for money!"

"Oh Ivy, how 'bout I give you money if you help me with chores

Like watering plants,

folding clothes,

and mopping floors."

Ivy said yes and had oh so much fun.
Time flew by and before she knew it, she was done!

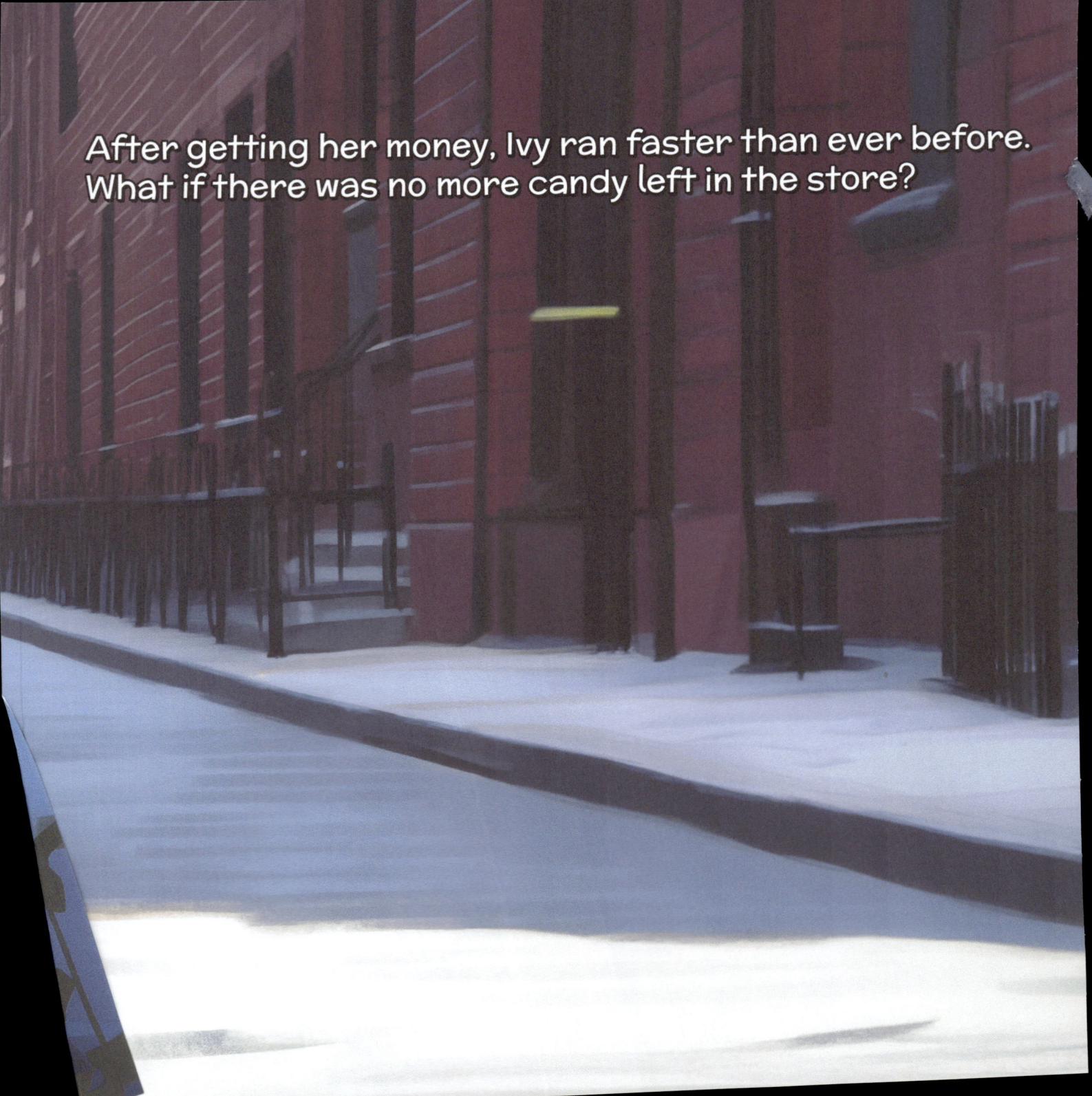

After getting her money, Ivy ran faster than ever before. What if there was no more candy left in the store?

On the way, she noticed a green piece of paper on the ground.
She picked it up and was surprised by what she had found.

It was more money than she had ever seen.
Suddenly she was richer than a queen.

Roaming the store she grabbed all she could take,
Things that make mouths happy and bellies to ache.

After her shopping spree was over,
She still had a good deal of money left over.

The next week, Mom said to Ivy, "Come try on what I got you.
It's a garden hat! Now you'll have one too!"

Then Ivy said bye and went out the door.
Outside she stopped by each shop buying goodies galore.

Her life and her stomach were swirled.
Flying in the sky, she screamed "I'm queen of the world!"

Mom looked on and let out a sigh.

She ran back to that old lucky place and combed the ground.
Sadly, there wasn't a penny to be found.

At the bank, no money came out of the machine.
The only thing to do was scream at the screen.

With throat so sore, she inspected the leaves on all of the trees.
But, no money had grown so she closed her eyes and said "Please".

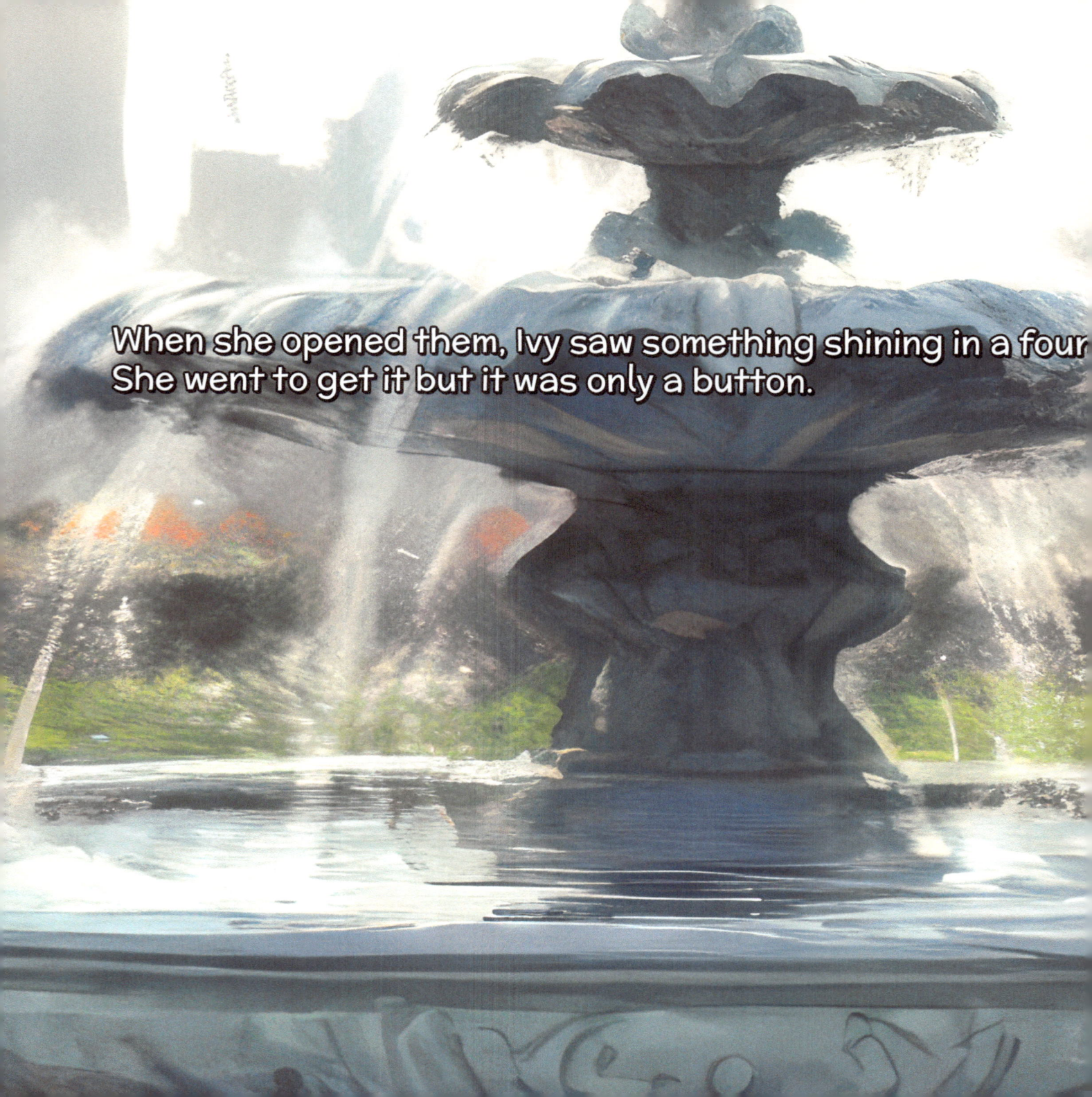

When she opened them, Ivy saw something shining in a four
She went to get it but it was only a button.

So soaked and so sad,
She thought of what she once had.

Just then, Mom put the basket on the edge of the table,
But it fell down because it wasn't stable.

"Oh no", said Mom with a strange smile on her face.
"I've gone and spilled the clothes all over the place."

Ivy didn't hesitate. "Sit back Mom! I'll take care of this mess!
Don't forget step three! Clean up to give yourself stress!"

Learn more about step three in "Ivy Spilled Milk"

Then every week after, Ivy helped Mom as best as she could.
She also saved all her money like she thought she should.

Ivy said to Mom, "Sorry for not spending time with you all those times before."

Mom said to Ivy, "Don't worry. I'll always be here for you. That's what moms are for."

Find money! Rate this book.

Please rate this book on Amazon. Typically only 1 in 100 people rate books and only 1 in 1,000 leave a review. Reviews for this book will increase the chances of your children finding money on the ground. If philanthropists end up reading this book, they would be absolutely compelled to leave money where children can find it. After all, the biggest takeaway from this book is that kids will learn valuable life lessons after coming across large amounts of money. Like Ivy, it'll lead them on an adventure that will ultimately have them return home to do chores. After that, butterflies will start filling gardens. If you like money, kids cleaning houses and butterflies, then rate this book.

Go to this book's Amazon webpage by using the QR code or by going to AlexanderSun.com/butterflies. There you'll find a button that takes you to Amazon. Flowers that get pollinated by butterflies thank you.

The story behind this book

Mr. Sun was really excited to write a story about this parable because it has lessons not only for children but also for parents as well. Funny enough, Mr. Sun had a hard time figuring out how he'd write it. Initially he was thinking of multiple animals like "Six Against the Slow & Steady" and "The Good Samaritan's Cat" but struggled. He thought about it for weeks but just couldn't find a way to get things to work so he focused on other stories to write. When he told his kids about his struggle, they immediately said to make it an Ivy book. The thought hadn't occurred to Mr. Sun because he was so fixated on animals and also because he hadn't thought about writing another Ivy book for a long time. It sounds strange but going through creative processes is often strange and frustrating.

About Mr. Sun

Mr. Sun's full name is Alexander Sun. He was born near San Francisco and later moved near LA to work at a video game company, Blizzard Entertainment. Growing up, Mr. Sun had a difficult time forgiving himself and others. He struggled with this problem for a long time and it wasn't until college did he learn to really let things go. After feeling the mental and relational benefits, he can't imagine going back to how he once was. Mr. Sun does his best to teach his 2 boys, Nathan and Ryan, life lessons he's learned and writing books is one of those ways. Aside from writing, Mr. Sun enjoys going to the playground, playing UNO and building things with Legos.

Peek inside all of Mr. Sun's books

Read some pages from all of Mr. Sun's books at AlexanderSun.com.

© 2024 Alexander Sun

Milton Keynes UK
Ingram Content Group UK Ltd.
UKHW052204011124
450426UK00002B/4